Jim Chimp's Story

Jim Chimp's Story

Muriel Blaustein

SIMON & SCHUSTER BOOKS FOR YOUNG READERS

Published by Simon & Schuster

New York · London · Toronto · Sydney · Tokyo · Singapore

SIMON & SCHUSTER BOOKS FOR YOUNG READERS

Simon & Schuster Building, Rockefeller Center, 1230 Avenue of the Americas, New York, New York 10020. Copyright © 1992 by Muriel Blaustein. All rights reserved including the right of reproduction in whole or in part in any form. SIMON & SCHUSTER BOOKS FOR YOUNG READERS is a trademark of Simon & Schuster.

Designed by Lucille Chomowicz.

The text of this book is set in 17 point Trump Mediaeval.

The illustrations were done in colored marking pens.

Manufactured in the United States of America   10   9   8   7   6   5   4   3   2   1

Library of Congress Cataloging-in-Publication Data

Blaustein, Muriel. Jim Chimp's story / by Muriel Blaustein. Summary: Jim Chimp is terrified when called upon to come before his class and tell a story, but everyone loves the tale of adventure that he relates.   [1. Chimpanzees—Fiction.   2. Public speaking—Fiction.]   I. Title.   PZ7.B61625Ji   1992

[E]—dc20   CIP   91-18001

ISBN 0-671-74779-7

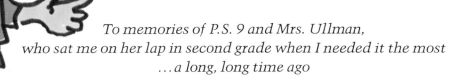

To memories of P.S. 9 and Mrs. Ullman,
who sat me on her lap in second grade when I needed it the most
...a long, long time ago

Jim Chimp was shy. He liked to sit in the last row in Mrs. Gibbon's class, hoping that the teacher would not call on him.

One day, Mrs. Gibbon said, "Wouldn't it be nice
if each of you told a story to the class? Jim Chimp,
would you come to the front of the room and be first?"

"Oh, no!"

"Come out, Jim," said Mrs. Gibbon.
I can't! thought Jim. Why, if I try to tell a story...

Jim dove under his desk.

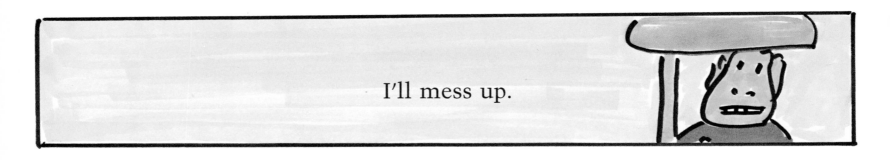

I'll mess up.

 Mrs. Gibbon will tell me to stay after class. She'll say, "Take your report card to the principal's office, Jim."

So I'll go to the principal's office. The principal will say, "No kid ever got an *F* in storytelling. You're suspended!"

So I'll go to cub scouts. The cub scout leader will say, "This weekend's our tepee campfire. Everyone is welcome—

except the kid who got the *F* in storytelling, Jim Chimp!"

 So I'll go home for my dinner. Dad will say, "How was school today, Jim?"

So I'll show him my report card. Dad will say, "I'm disappointed in you, son!"

And Mom will say, "What will your Grandma, Grandpa, Aunt Dot, Uncle Tony, and Cousin Bob say?"

 I'll be the only kid who doesn't get a present at Christmas. And I'll be sent to bed without a Christmas dinner.

The mayor will come to see me. He'll say, "We don't want you in our town, Jim!"

So I'll run away, and set sail to sea,

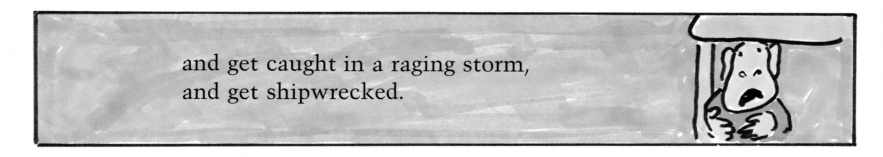

and get caught in a raging storm,
and get shipwrecked.

And a pirate will come along. "Ahoy!" he'll say. "Are you Jim Chimp, who got the *F* in storytelling?"

So he'll take me back to his ship and say, "Swab the deck! Polish my boots! Fix the rigging! And when you're done—*walk the plank!*"

That'll be the last straw! I'll say, "Is *that* so?"
I'll reach up and take the pirate by surprise.
"You walk the plank!"

And the pirate will listen.
I'll pull him in with a rope and tie him up.

And I'll steer for home.
"Tell the mayor I'm here," I'll say.

The mayor will have a ceremony. "We award Jim
Chimp this medal of honor for bravery."

 Mom will ask, "Pumpkin or mince pie?"
Dad will add, "Wait till you see your Christmas presents!"

The cub scout leader will let me lead the troops up the trail. "Wait for us, Jim!"

 At school the principal will meet me at the door.

And in class

I'll come out from under my desk
to tell my story just as I imagined it....

And Jim Chimp did!

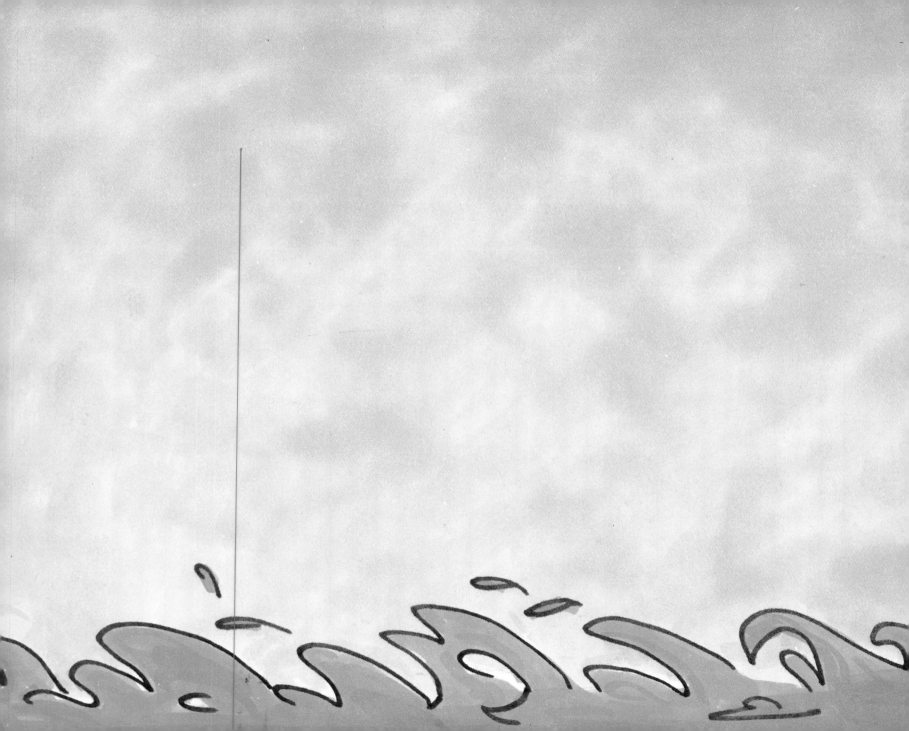